Billionaire's Nanny Fake Marriage

Lilly Grace Nash

Published by JL Lam Publishing, 2024.

This is a work of fiction. Similarities to real people, places, or events are entirely coincidental.

BILLIONAIRE'S NANNY FAKE MARRIAGE

First edition. May 9, 2024.

Copyright © 2024 Lilly Grace Nash.

ISBN: 979-8227446657

Written by Lilly Grace Nash.

Also by Lilly Grace Nash

SEALs of Love Romance
Undercover Hearts

Standalone
Alliances & Betrayals
Billionaire's Nanny Fake Marriage

Watch for more at https://lillygracenash.com.

Table of Contents

To my beloved husband,

whose unwavering support, endless encouragement,

and steadfast belief in me

have been the guiding light throughout my journey.

Your love is the foundation upon which I build my dreams.

Jackson

Jackson leaned back in the plush leather chair in his executive office atop the gleaming Thornfield Towers, headquarters of Thornfield, Rutledge and Madison; Attorneys-at-Law. As senior partner, the coveted corner office was fitting for a man of his stature.

"For the last time Mother, I don't have time to go out with Clarissa Von Brockton," Jackson said in exasperation, loosening his Armani tie.

"But Jackson, dear, she comes from an excellent family and is such a pretty girl. I just want my only son to find a nice wife and settle down. You spend all your time at that dreary old office!" His mother's voice rang through the phone.

Jackson ran a hand through his dark hair. If only she knew that 'dreary old office' had been in their esteemed family for three generations, making them one of the most influential families in Savannah high society.

"I know you mean well, but right now my priority is Lily," Jackson said, his voice softening at the mention of his beloved six-year-old daughter. He would move heaven and earth for that little girl ever since his wife Melissa passed away two years ago.

"Lily needs a mother figure. You can't shelter her forever," his mother insisted.

"I should get going. Tell Father hello for me," Jackson said, eager to end this tiresome conversation. His mother meant well but couldn't resist meddling in his love life.

As he gazed out the floor-to-ceiling windows overlooking the Savannah skyline, Jackson loosened his collar. Lily would be home from school soon. He lived for their evenings together, where he could shed the pressures that came with the Thornfield name and legacy.

Straightening his tailored three-piece suit, Jackson strode out of his stately office, sleek leather briefcase in hand. As he walked through the bustling hallways of Thornfield Towers, his employees nodded respectfully, parting ways for the formidable senior partner.

Outside, his driver opened the door of the shiny black Mercedes, which whisked Jackson out of the city and to his mansion near the shores of the Atlantic Ocean. The entire ride, one thought consumed Jackson's mind: Lily.

His sweet, precious daughter depended on him for everything. Jackson had vowed not to fail her. No matter what expectations his family and Savannah society placed on him, Lily would always come first.

For now, his little girl with her golden curls and sparkling green eyes was all the family Jackson needed. Her infectious laughter and unconditional love filled his heart in a way nothing else could.

After kissing her mother's photo each night, Jackson would tuck Lily into bed with a story and a prayer. Those quiet moments together were the balm that soothed his soul after long days at the office. Lily gave him purpose amidst the pressures and chaos.

Come what may, Jackson would move heaven and earth to make sure his daughter was safe, happy, and loved. She was his most precious gift, his guiding light. With Lily by his side, he could weather any storm.

***

He used to make it a priority to be home when Lily returned from school, eager to hear about her day over milk and cookies. But now Jackson found himself stuck at the office more nights than not, poring over legal briefs into the wee hours. Just last week, he'd missed Lily's dance recital, something he deeply regretted.

It pained Jackson to think of Lily returning home each day with just staff there. As much as he tried adjusting his schedule, he couldn't be in two places at once.

He knew his parents adored their precious granddaughter, but they had made it clear they were too busy to help regularly. His mother volunteered on several prominent charity boards, while his father spent many days on the golf course with clients. Their calendar was overwhelmed with social engagements.

"We wish we could see Lily more often, but our schedule is just out of control!" his mother had said apologetically over lunch last month. "We can try to visit when we're in town. You know, if you would just find a wife, you wouldn't have to worry about Lily so much."

Jackson knew their intentions were good. They always made a fuss over Lily on holidays, showering her with affection and gifts. But the rest of the year, their focus remained fixed on the country club scene.

As far as Jackson's parents were concerned, hands-on childcare was the responsibility of hired help. They came from a generation that valued nannies raising children. Still, Jackson hoped they would make Lily more of a priority.

He tried not to resent their busyness. After all, they had raised him well while building their family law firm and their status in Savannah high society. But Jackson longed for them to truly know and embrace their only grandchild.

Lily deserved grandparents who didn't just swoop in on special occasions, but who were a constant, loving presence in her life. Jackson could never replace that unique bond.

Perhaps it was time to hire a nanny, he pondered. It would allow Lily to have someone at home when he got tied up at work. And it might get his mother off his back about spending every free minute with her. Surely, he could find someone qualified yet trustworthy.

Glancing at a picture of Lily on his desk, Jackson made up his mind. He would speak to his HR department first thing in the morning about vetting potential nannies. His little princess deserved to have someone care for her when he couldn't be there himself. Even if it meant relinquishing control, it was the right thing to do.

True to his word, Jackson had HR compile a list of qualified nanny candidates first thing Monday morning. He wanted only the best for his precious Lily.

Throughout the week, Jackson conducted interviews during lunch and between client meetings. While the nannies came with glowing recommendations and experience, he struggled to find the perfect match for Lily.

Stacy was not very rigid about schedules and routines. Jamie came off as immature. Mrs. Smith reminded him too much of his uptight grandmother. Each candidate was missing that special something, that spark.

By Friday afternoon, Jackson felt ready to give up hope after yet another lackluster interview. He loosened his tie and sighed, glancing at the one remaining name on his schedule: Emma Turner. She was likely just another dud.

"Send in the last one," Jackson grumbled to his secretary. Moments later, a petite brunette with kind eyes and a bright smile entered.

Jackson scowled as the last candidate of the day, Emma Turner, walked into his office. He loosened his collar in irritation and gestured for her to sit.

"Let's make this quick, I'm a busy man," Jackson grumbled. "What makes you qualified to care for my daughter?"

Emma held her chin high, unfazed by Jackson's brusque demeanor. "With over 10 years of childcare experience, I'm extremely qualified. My background in early childhood education and glowing references speak for themselves."

Jackson blinked, surprised by her confidence. The other applicants had wilted under his stern questioning.

Over the next thirty minutes, Jackson tried to find cracks in Emma's polished exterior, but she held her ground. She asked thoughtful questions about Lily's schedule, interests, and needs. Her creativity and problem-solving impressed Jackson, though he refused to show it.

"I'll need to see how you interact with Lily before making a decision," Jackson said bluntly, expecting Emma to balk at the extra demand.

Instead, Emma smiled brightly. "Of course! I look forward to spending time with her and demonstrating my capabilities."

Jackson raised an eyebrow, finding Emma difficult to intimidate. She met his gaze without flinching.

"Very well then, this weekend it is," Jackson agreed gruffly. He had a feeling Emma could handle anything he or Lily threw her way. And for the first time that week, he felt a spark of hope.

Emma

I step into the opulent Thornfield Mansion, my heart pounding with anticipation and nerves. This is it—the beginning of my new job as Lily Thornfield's nanny. Taking a deep breath, I remind myself to be confident and poised, despite the jitters that threaten to betray me.

As I make my way through the grand foyer, my eyes take in the exquisite marble floors, the sparkling chandeliers casting a soft glow, and the overall grandeur that defines the Thornfield residence. It's a sight to behold, but it also adds to my apprehension. Can I handle this? I can't afford to mess this up—I need this job to pay my bills.

Suddenly, a voice interrupts my thoughts, its tone dripping with annoyance. "Miss Turner." I turn to face the source of the voice. Standing before me is Jackson Thornfield himself, the enigmatic billionaire and my boss. His eyes, a stormy gray, bore into mine; his arms crossed over his chest, exuding an air of authority that sends shivers down my spine.

"Good morning, Mr. Thornfield." My voice is laced with determination. I refuse to back down in the face of his overwhelming presence. I know my worth, and I won't let his attitude diminish it.

Jackson's lips curl into a slight smirk, a mix of amusement and skepticism. "We'll see if you're up to the task," he retorts dismissively. The tension between us is palpable, and I can practically feel the electricity crackling in the air.

Annoyed by his condescending tone, I push back. "I assure you, Mr. Thornfield, I am more than capable of caring for Lily.

My qualifications speak for themselves." My voice is steady, even though my insides churn with frustration.

Jackson raises an eyebrow, clearly unimpressed. "We'll see." His tone is laced with skepticism. "Lily is my priority. If you can't handle it, you can leave."

Leave? The mere suggestion stirs a fire within me. I need this job, and I refuse to let Jackson Thornfield chase me away so easily. I square my shoulders and meet his piercing gaze head-on. "I didn't come here just to walk away." Unyielding determination is evident in my voice.

His gaze lingers on me for a moment, assessing my resolve. Then, finally, he grudgingly nods. "Fine. You should meet Lily. Follow me."

I can't help but feel a sense of victory. The resentment within me begins to bud, like a small seed of defiance against Jackson's dismissive attitude. I may have won this round, but I can sense that there will be future altercations.

As Mr. Thornfield briskly led me through the grand mansion, admiration and intimidation vied within me. The sprawling rooms dripped with opulence - marble floors, crystal chandeliers, ornate furnishings. I smoothed my simple cotton dress, feeling out of place.

Mr. Thornfield retained a formal distance as he perfunctorily explained Lily's schedule and preferences. After outlining her routines, he paused, considering his words.

"Miss Turner, I believe some transparency is warranted regarding my family's expectations," he began. "While I make hiring decisions for my own household, my parents are rather particular about who associates with us."

He cleared his throat delicately. "To be frank, they will likely question your suitability upon learning of your...non-traditional background. However, they do not yet know I have hired you. I merely wanted you to be prepared for biased judgments from them."

I processed this carefully, touched by his honesty. "Thank you for informing me, Mr. Thornfield. I appreciate you inviting me into your home regardless of tradition," I replied. "While I cannot change others' assumptions, I hope to prove myself on the basis of merit, care and dedication over time. Lily's well being will always be my priority."

Mr. Thornfield appraised me anew, seemingly satisfied by my tactful yet principled response. With a brusque nod, he resumed the tour. I held my head high, refusing to be intimidated. Their elite world may be new, but caring for children was not. That would be my guiding purpose.

I follow Jackson Thornfield through the elegant halls of his mansion until we reach a room filled with toys and soft pastel colors. Lily's room, I presume. My heart flutters with a mixture of excitement and nervousness as I catch a glimpse of the little girl whose life I will become a significant part of.

"Lily, sweetheart, meet Miss Emma. She'll be taking care of you from now on while I am at work." Jackson's voice holds a hint of tenderness I hadn't noticed before as he introduces me to his daughter.

Lily's eyes widen with curiosity as she takes in my presence, and a wide smile graces her cherubic face. "Hi, Miss Emma!" Her small arms reach out to me in invitation.

The sight of her infectious joy melts away any remaining reservations I had about this job. I crouch down to her level and open my arms, welcoming her embrace. "Hello, Lily." My voice carries a hint of genuine warmth. "I'm so excited to be here with you."

Jackson watches our interaction, a flicker of surprise crossing his features. The love between father and daughter is evident in the way he gazes at Lily, and it seems he's found comfort in witnessing her instant connection with me.

A smile tugs at the corners of his lips, softening his stern countenance. "It looks like you've won her over." His remark came in a soft tone.

I met his gaze with a sense of triumph in my eyes. "Lily is a remarkable little girl. I promise to take good care of her," I assure him earnestly.

A moment passes, filled with unspoken understanding, before Jackson finally nods. "Alright, Emma. You have the job. Lily's happiness is my priority," he concedes, gratitude tinged in his voice.

As I rise to my feet, I feel a sense of relief and gratitude wash over me. Lily's acceptance has granted me not only the job but also a chance to prove myself to Jackson. I know the road ahead won't be easy, but this small victory fuels my determination to succeed.

With Lily's hand securely in mine, I turn to face Jackson, a newfound respect shining in my eyes. "Thank you, Mr. Thornfield. You won't be disappointed." I squeeze Lily's hand slightly, my voice filled with quiet confidence.

Before Jackson can say anything, his phone rings, abruptly interrupting the brief moment of peace. His face tightens as he listens intently to the caller on the other end, his brows furrowing with concern.

"Hello? What's the situation? I see, yes, I'll be right there," his voice is clipped and filled with urgency.

Realizing that time is of the essence, Jackson hurriedly strides toward the grand entrance, his phone still glued to his ears. As though by instinct, I follow him. Watching him step out of the house, I realize he did not give me any instructions regarding his daughter or his house.

I hastily called out after him, "Wait, Mr. Thornfield! Before you go, are there any special rules or routines I should know about?"

His steps falter, and his gaze lingers on me, but the urgency of the situation takes precedence. Without a word, he hops into his car, leaving my question hanging in the air, unanswered.

I watch as his sleek black sports car—a testament to his success—roars to life, the engine's powerful growl filling the tranquil atmosphere. Its polished exterior glistens under the sunlight, the wheels gliding smoothly over the paved ground.

As the car disappears into the distance, a pang of disappointment settles in my chest. The unanswered question nags at me, but I shake off the unease. I can figure things out on my own. I'm resourceful, and Lily will guide me in her own way.

Just as I turn to head back inside, a gentle tug on my hand interrupts my thoughts. I look down to see Lily, her bright eyes sparkling with anticipation. She lets out an excited giggle, urging me to follow.

"Miss Emma, come play with me! Let's have a tea party!" Lily exclaims, brimming with childlike enthusiasm.

Her invitation warms my heart, and I can't resist the infectious joy radiating from her. "Of course, Lily! Lead the way,"

I say, allowing myself to be drawn back into the house, ready to embark on this whimsical adventure.

Her tiny fingers guide me through the door and into her playroom—a kaleidoscope of colors with toys strewn across the floor. Stuffed animals and building blocks create a fanciful landscape, while a small table set with miniature tea cups await our pretend tea party.

Lily's boundless enthusiasm is contagious as we settle down, filling our cups and engaging in animated conversations with the stuffed panda and unicorn guests, and I'm reminded of the enchanting bond that can form between a child and a caregiver.

Jackson

I sit behind my imposing ornate desk, watching as Emma scans through the meticulously detailed document—a compilation of instructions, rules, and regulations she is expected to follow as Lily's nanny. The list covers everything from Lily's dietary preferences to her bedtime routine, with precise instructions on playtime, outings, and even the clothes she should wear.

As essential as it is that Lily's care is meticulously organized, a part of me wonders if I've gone too far. However, my protective instincts kick in, and I can't help but feel the need to shield my daughter from any potential harm.

"Mr. Thornfield, this... this is quite extensive." She stammers, trying to maintain her composure.

I lean back in my chair, my expression stoic. "Lily's well-being is of utmost importance to me. These guidelines ensure she remains safe and happy."

Emma glances through the list again, then looks up, her gaze meeting mine. "I understand the need for structure, Mr. Thornfield, but Lily also needs the freedom to explore and learn through her own experiences."

I narrow my eyes at her, my voice sharp. "I appreciate your concern, Miss Turner, but I know what's best for my daughter."

She takes a deep breath, gliding her tongue over her lips. "With all due respect, Mr. Thornfield, Lily needs more than just rules. She needs love, laughter, and the freedom to be herself. Trust me, I've worked with children before, and they thrive when given the opportunity to discover the world around them."

A flicker of vulnerability courses through me as her words touch a nerve. Then, in a soft but firm tone, she adds, "I'm not saying we should abandon structure completely, but perhaps we can find a balance—a way to incorporate your guidelines while allowing Lily to explore her own interests and develop her own personality."

My guarded heart tightens at her words, and for a moment, silence hangs in the air, tension coiling between us. Then a small sigh escapes my lips, and I lean forward, my hands clasped on the desk.

"You don't understand, Miss Turner," I say, aware of the touch of sadness that tinges my voice. "I've seen firsthand the pain that comes when trust is shattered."

I go on to explain about Lily's last nanny Claire who left without notice. "Lily was devastated. She didn't understand why Claire would leave without even saying goodbye. As you can see from your first meeting with Lily, she's a very trusting child. I can't put her through that again."

Emma's eyes fill with empathy as she listens. "Trust takes time to rebuild when it's been broken. But we'll take it slowly, and I'll prove myself through my actions. Lily deserves that chance. You both do."

Her voice carries a tone of compassionate professionalism. I appreciate her validation of my concerns and her patience.

"Thank you for understanding, Miss Turner. With time and care, I hope we can forge new beginnings built on trust. But it won't happen overnight after our experiences."

Emma gives a kind nod. "Of course, Mr. Thornfield. We'll go at your pace and do what's best for Lily." huluEmma's eyes soften, and her firm voice is gentle. "I promise to do everything I can to ensure Lily's safety and happiness. But part of that happiness comes from allowing her to experience the world, to make her own choices, and to learn from them. Together, we can create an environment where Lily feels loved, protected, and encouraged to explore. It won't be easy, but it will be worth it."

I pause, contemplating her words. There's an unwavering determination in Emma's eyes—a genuine desire to help Lily grow. Maybe, just maybe, there's a way to find a balance—a middle ground that keeps Lily safe without stifling her spirit.

After a moment, I lean back in my chair with a nod, a silent agreement passing between us. "Alright, Miss Turner. Let's find that balance—for Lily's sake."

"Thank you, Mr. Thornfield." Emma rises, exiting my home office.

****

Days pass, and Lily settles into a familiar routine under Emma's watchful care. I'm grateful for Emma's unwavering dedication to Lily's well-being, but a seed of doubt lingers within me. It sprouts one evening when a sudden crash pierces the tranquility of our home.

In a state of alarm, I rush into the living room, my heart pounding. There, I find Lily standing near a shattered vase, her innocent eyes wide with fear. Emma stands nearby, her expression clouded with regret.

The moment I saw the shattered vase on the floor, panic seized me. I rush over and scoop Lily into my arms, checking her small body for any sign of injury. Relief floods me as I confirm she is unharmed, but my protective instincts remain on high alert.

I turn to Emma, unable to contain the swell of disappointment rising within me. "How could you let this happen?" I ask, my voice sharp.

Emma's face falls. "It was an accident, I only looked away for a moment..." she starts to explain, distress evident in her tone.

"No excuses!" I interject, my imagination running wild with what could have transpired. "You were irresponsible and left my daughter in harm's way."

Emma opens her mouth as if to respond, but I silence her with a stern look. The fury coursing through me leaves no room for discussion.

"I trusted you with my daughter, and you betrayed that trust," I continue, my words biting. Lily looks between us, her little brow creased in confusion.

Shaking my head, I say with chilling calmness, "I'm deeply disappointed right now. This is unacceptable."

Emma withers under my harsh scrutiny, but I am unrelenting. When it comes to Lily's safety, I have zero tolerance for negligence.

As I turn away, cradling Lily against my chest, Emma calls out in despair, "Mr. Thornfield, please, it was just a mistake, I promise it won't happen again..."

"Daddy?" Lily's voice quivers, casting a glance between me and Emma.

My anger momentarily subsides as I witness Lily on the verge of tears. Guilt begins to seep into my heart, realizing that my reaction may have been excessive. Softening my tone, a mix of regret and concern tinges my voice.

"I'm sorry, Emma. I did not mean to lash out."

Emma reaches out, and Lily instinctively wraps her tiny arms around her. "I understand, Mr. Thornfield. Lily means the world to you, and I should have been more cautious."

"I'm sorry, Miss Emma," Lily murmurs, stroking Emma's face tenderly.

"It's okay, princess. Accidents happen, and we can learn from them. As long as you are not hurt, it's okay. I'll clean up the mess right away." Emma reassures Lily with a tender pat on the back. Her affectionate gesture triggers a bittersweet pang in my heart, a poignant reminder of the loving moments I will never share with my late wife.

I watch as Emma's care and attention bring a smile back to Lily's face. The sight warms my heart, easing the lingering traces of anger and frustration. In that moment, I realize the significance of Emma's presence in our lives—a source of comfort and stability for Lily; and a beacon of hope for a future I had once believed to be impossible.

"Thank you, Emma. Sometimes, my fears get the best of me. Come on, Lily. Let's make sure you're not hurt and get you changed." With Lily securely in my arms, I take her to her room while Emma retrieves a broom to clean up the floor.

Emma

I can barely contain my excitement when Lily rushes in exclaiming she was picked for the school showcase. My heart swells and I give her a big hug. "That's wonderful! I'm so proud of you," I say.

Over the next few weeks, I help Lily prepare for the big event. We work on creative costumes and props for the interactive presentation she plans to give. Her enthusiasm as I support her is contagious.

On the big day, I help Lily carefully load everything into the car before Mr. Thornfield drives us to the school. My fingers tingle with anticipation on the drive over. I can't wait to see Lily's hard work come to fruition.

At the school, Lily hugs her dad then scampers off to meet her classmates. Mr. Thornfield and I take our seats in the auditorium. I smooth my dress, wanting to look nice for Lily's moment.

The show begins and each student presents their unique act. Finally, Lily's name is called. She waves at us before launching into her creative performance. I have to dab my eyes, I feel so proud of her.

Afterwards, Lily throws her arms around me in a big hug. "Thank you for your help!" she exclaims. On the drive home, her contagious joy fills the car.

I share a smile with Mr. Thornfield, our hearts full of pride for Lily. Being part of this special event as her nanny meant so much to me. I cherish our growing bond and can't wait for the next adventure.

The excitement from Lily's successful showcase spilled over into the entire drive home. From her carseat in the back, she chattered nonstop to Mr. Thornfield and I about every detail of her presentation and the audience's reactions.

"Did you see when I made the volcano explode glitter, Daddy? Everyone said it was so cool!" she exclaimed.

"Absolutely, princess. The glitter was a perfect touch," Mr. Thornfield replied warmly. Lily's enthusiasm was contagious.

"Oh, and when I got everyone to do the rainforest animal dance with me? The monkeys were so funny!" Lily giggled as she reminisced.

"You definitely got the audience involved, sweetie. All your elements were wonderful," I added supportively. Her creativity had shone so brightly on stage today.

The smile on Lily's face was one of pure joy and accomplishment. After weeks of diligent preparation, seeing her hard work pay off filled me with pride. She completely came out of her shell up there.

As we pulled into the driveway, Lily begged her dad to let her watch the video he'd recorded of her performance again. "Please Daddy, pleeease can we show Miss Emma? I wanna see it again!"

Mr. Thornfield and I shared an amused smile at her infectious delight. "Of course, honey." Lily's happiness meant everything today.

After the exhilaration of Lily's school showcase, I can tell the day's events have left her far too wired and excited to go straight to sleep. As we go through her usual bedtime routine, her eyes remain bright and alert despite the late hour.

I read Lily her favorite fairy tales, then suggest warm milk to help her unwind. But even after two bedtime stories, she still seems wide awake, recounting every detail of her presentation and the applause she received.

Finally, I decide to sing her lullabies, hoping the soothing melodies will lull her to sleep. I make sure to choose slow, peaceful songs, gently stroking her hair as I sing. Sometimes multiple lullabies are needed to help her finally relax after an exciting day.

Eventually Lily's excited chattering dies down as my singing works its magic. Her eyelids grow heavy and her grip on her stuffed unicorn slackens. After four lullabies, her breathing becomes deep and even - she's drifted off to sleep at last.

I quietly turn out the lights and leave her to peaceful dreams, grateful this overstimulated child is finally getting some rest. I feel exhausted after the long day and difficult winding down process.

Heading downstairs, I find Mr. Thornfield waiting in the living room as he often does in the evenings. But tonight, he seems anxious and on edge rather than his usual calm, collected self. My curiosity grows as he invites me to sit. What could be weighing so heavily on his mind after such a joyful day?

"Miss Turner, I have an important matter to discuss with you," he begins nervously. "I just received a call from my mother. She is insisting I bring a serious girlfriend to their 50th anniversary gala in January."

He goes on to explain that his parents host a grand affair annually at their estate on St. Simons Island, where his mother uses it as an opportunity to try and pair him with women she deems suitable.

"She's constantly attempting to play matchmaker at these events, despite my protests," he says, a hint of exasperation in his tone. "No matter how many casual dates I've brought over the years, it's never enough for her."

He runs his hands through his hair in frustration as he recounts his mother's relentless antics. I listen with empathy, but uncertainty stirs in me about where this is leading.

Mr. Thornfield turns to me then, his eyes now hesitant, even nervous. "Miss Turner, I have a massive, inappropriate favor to ask of you. Feel free to turn me down, but you're my last hope."

I brace myself, unclear what kind of request could make him so unsure. He takes a deep breath before finally blurting out, "Would you consider pretending to be my fiancée for the anniversary gala? It's the only way to convince my mother to give me some space."

I stare at Mr. Thornfield in stunned silence, certain I must have misheard him. But the earnest look in his eyes confirms it - he just asked me, the nanny, to pretend to be his fiancée. I feel lightheaded as I attempt to process the implications of this unexpected request.

"Let me get this straight," I begin slowly. "You want me...to pretend to be your fiancée...at your parents' anniversary gala?"

Mr. Thornfield nods solemnly. "I know it's highly unusual. But my mother is relentless in her attempts to find me a wife. If I show up alone, she'll be devastated and set me up with whatever socialite's daughter she pleases. This is the only way."

I pace the room, emotions swirling wildly. "But sir, don't you see how risky this could be? Falsely leading your parents to believe we have a serious relationship goes against my better judgment."

I voice my deepest concern. "Most worryingly, if this charade was ever found out, it could ruin my reputation and cost me my position here. I care about you and Lily too much to jeopardize that."

Mr. Thornfield steps forward. "Emma, I would never put you in harm's way. This would be a performance only, no one would ever know the truth."

His eyes are pleading, his voice edged with desperation. "You're the only one I trust for this. It would just be for one night, we'd announce a fake engagement then after the gala I'd say we split up amicably." He looks at me beseechingly.

I feel my resistance wavering as I search his gaze. Could I really agree to this risky proposition? My heart and head wage war, uncertain if either choice leads to smooth waters ahead.

Part of me sympathizes with his difficult position with his parents' expectations. But engaging in such an intimate ruse could irreversibly complicate my professional relationship with him and his family.

When he insists it's the only way to satisfy his mother, I choose my next words extremely carefully. "I'm honored you would entrust me with this, but are you certain there isn't a better option? Falsely leading your parents on seems morally questionable. I worry this could put both of us in an untenable situation."

I voice my biggest concern. "Most of all, I'm unsure of how pretending to be your fiancée could impact my position working here. I care deeply for you and Lily and don't want to jeopardize that."

Mr. Thornfield nods solemnly, validating my hesitations. We proceed to discuss the matter from all angles - the risks, the alternatives, Lily's well being. I make it clear that if I agree to this scheme, we would need to establish very clear boundaries to avoid blurred lines.

After much difficult discussion, we reach a tentative understanding. But uncertainty lingers in me - have we made the best choice, or could this spiral in unpredictable ways? Only time will tell...

Jackson

The excitement and pride from Lily's school showcase stays with me on the ride home. Seeing my daughter up on that stage, eyes shining with joy, was a memory I'll cherish forever.

I am downstairs listening to Emma and Lily upstairs. Emma is singing lullabies to Lilly. My contented reverie is interrupted by the jarring ringtone I've set for my mother. I know whatever she's calling about can't be good. With a resigned sigh, I answer.

"Jackson, dear! How lovely to catch you," she trills in her artificially sweet voice that sets my teeth on edge. I hum noncommittally, bracing myself for whatever new meddling or judgment she's decided upon today.

"Now, I'm calling about preparations for the gala. Your father and I expect you to be there, no excuses," she continues. Of course, their 50th anniversary gala, the social event of the season. How could I forget my duties to put in a good appearance and schmooze with Savannah's elites?

Mother clears her throat, a sure sign she's about to deliver unwelcome news. "I won't beat around the bush. You simply must bring a proper date this year. I'm tired of you distracting all the eligible young ladies, stag at every event!"

I squeeze my eyes shut and pinch the bridge of my nose, attempting to restrain my frustration. "I've told you before, I'm quite content being on my own right now. My priority is caring for Lily."

"Nonsense!" she interjects in horror. "Don't you want your daughter to have a mother figure? You need to find a suitable wife, and I have just the woman..."

I clench my jaw as she prattles on about Laura Huntsburg being an ideal match. Like I'm some prize bull she wants to mate with fine stock.

After what feels like endless harping, Mother finally concludes her tirade with an ultimatum — either I show up with a serious romantic partner on my arm, or she'll take matters into her own hands. The threat makes my blood run cold. Engaged to a near stranger just to uphold the family image? I can't allow that to happen.

So after hurried goodbyes, I go to the one person I think can help me - Emma. I approach her hesitantly once Lily is tucked into bed. "Miss Turner, I have an immense favor to ask, and it's quite irregular..."

I explain the conversation with Mother and how I need to convince her I'm seriously involved with someone. Then I stammer the risky request, "Would you consider accompanying me to the gala as my pretend fiancée? Just for the one event, to get her off my back?"

Shock and hesitation flash across Emma's face. She immediately voices concerns over risking her reputation and relationship with our family. While valid worries, desperation claws inside me.

After thoughtful discussion, Emma reluctantly agrees to my scheme, as long as we establish boundaries. We'll announce a fake engagement at the gala, then afterwards inform my family we've ended it amicably.

I'm flooded with relief, thanking her profusely. I know how inappropriate this situation is, but feel backed into a corner. With Emma posing as my fiancée for the night, perhaps we can finally curb my mother's relentless matchmaking and demands.

Over the next weeks, we plan every detail. Of course Emma needs a dress for the black tie affair, so I arranged for a couture house to design something custom. I insist on covering all expenses, it's the least I can do.

As Emma and I delve into our meticulous preparations for pretending to be engaged, an unexpected tension slowly simmers between us. During our countless rehearsal sessions ironing out details, her feminine allure catches me unexpectedly off guard.

At first, it's little things - the pleasing melody of her laugh, the elegant slope of her neck as she brushes back a lock of hair. Brief moments I try to ignore, but linger in my thoughts nonetheless. Surely just attentiveness to selling our ruse, I rationalize.

Yet over weeks spent in close company, something imperceptible shifts. Our scripted interactions take on a charged subtext, sparked by playful banter and admiring glances that go beyond mere acting.

One evening, as we sit by the crackling fire practicing affectionate gazes, I find myself mesmerized by the golden glow of flames dancing across Emma's delicate features. The urge to reach out and caress her cheek becomes nearly overwhelming. I clench my hands tightly, forcing myself to refocus.

"Shall we run through our proposal story again?" I suggest briskly, attempting to break the hypnotic spell of the moment. Emma blinks as if emerging from a daydream, then nods agreeably. As she recites the sweet but fabricated tale, I study her intently.

When did this beguiling woman I hired as my daughter's nanny begin occupying so much of my awareness? I chalk it up to immersive preparation for our pretend betrothal and nothing more.

Yet during an afternoon stroll in the gardens, Emma suddenly turns to me. "Jackson, if you were to spontaneously kiss me in front of your mother, how should I respond? For appearances, of course."

Her bold inquiry catches me completely off guard. My mouth goes dry at the thought, and I take a slow breath to calm my sudden nerves. "I believe a shy smile followed by affectionately squeezing my arm would appear natural," I manage to reply. Emma nods thoughtfully and we resume walking, but my pulse continues to quicken.

At first, I don't think Lily notices the subtle shift occurring between Emma and myself. But over time, I catch her observing us with her curious, innocent eyes.

One evening at dinner, I compliment Emma's new hairstyle and she blushes attractively. I see Lily look back and forth between us, a knowing grin spreading across her face. Clearly my daughter is perceptive.

I've tried to be discreet, but Lily detects the admiring glances and whispers passing between myself and Emma. She watches us with joyful eyes, as if reminded of a fairy tale romance.

Though we attempt to conceal our growing affections, it's clear my daughter recognizes the shift. I suppose it was naive to think we could hide it from someone who knows us both so well.

Perhaps I should feel self-conscious at the thought of Lily observing my unfolding feelings toward Emma. But instead, her delight over our blossoming closeness puts me at ease. All Lily wants is for the two people she loves most to find happiness together.

One rainy evening at home, I decided we should practice dancing to convincingly play the part of newly engaged sweethearts. As we waltz slowly around the ballroom, Emma's hand delicately clasped in mine, the feeling of her body swaying close against me stirred undeniable desire. I quickly step back, mumbling apologies for treading on her foot.

Later, as I undress for bed, my mind continues replaying images of Emma's luminous eyes gazing up at me, her hand resting lightly on my shoulder, her sweet lips turned up in a faint smile. Abruptly shaking my head, I splash cold water on my face in frustration.

This captivating woman was hired to care for Lily, not ignite forbidden passion within me. I must regain composure and control before the gala arrives and our performance begins. Any longing I feel surely stems from immersing myself too thoroughly in this fabricated romance.

At night, my dreams betray my attempts at denial, filled with heated embraces and hungry kisses that dissolve into disappointment come morning light. I throw myself into work and final party preparations, trying to quell my conflicted mind.

The night of the gala finally arrives in a swirl of anticipation and anxiety. As Emma and I ride to the glamorous hotel where the event is being held, I notice her wringing her hands, clearly nervous. Without thinking, I place my hand over hers reassuringly.

"It's all going to be alright," I murmur. Emma's eyes meet mine, and she gives a small, unconvincing smile in return, my hand still covering hers. Realizing my forwardness, I swiftly pull back, turning to gaze out the window for the remainder of the ride.

We have a performance to get through tonight. But as we prepare to step out and announce our engagement to Savannah's scrutinizing elite, a small voice in my head wonders - how much longer until this pretense becomes my new reality? I quickly silence it, offering Emma my arm as we enter the opulent ballroom and leave caution behind for the night.

Emma

I smooth the elegant fabric of my dress, my hands shaking slightly as I take a final appraising look in the floor length mirror. Tonight is the night of the momentous gala, where I must pretend to be Jackson's fiancée in front of his entire prestigious family. The thought makes my stomach churn with anxiety.

When Jackson first proposed this elaborate ruse, I naively thought I could handle it. But now, preparing to deceive people, I feel racked with guilt. Lily and Jackson have become family to me this past year and I am beginning to have feelings for Jackson that are not just fake. Yet here I am, about to put on a performance that could jeopardize everything we've built if discovered.

A gentle knock on the door stirs me from my spiraling thoughts. I open it to find Jackson standing there, handsome as ever in his tailored tuxedo. But his usual confidence seems clouded by the same apprehension swirling within me.

"The car is waiting downstairs whenever you're ready," he says. But in his eyes, I see the unspoken question - are we really ready for this?

I take a deep breath and nod, clutching my gilded clutch. "I just need another minute." Closing the door, I smooth my dress once more and check my hair in the mirror. The illusion must be perfect tonight.

Settling into the plush leather seat of the sleek town car, I gaze out the tinted windows as we make our way from Jackson's lavish beachfront neighborhood toward the historic Savannah country club where the gala is being held.

My pulse quickens as we pull up to the sprawling columned venue. This is Jackson's world, not mine. Tonight I must try to blend in as if I truly belong.

Escorted by liveried servers, we enter the grand ballroom. Chandeliers bathe the space in golden light while an orchestra plays softly. Extravagantly dressed guests sip cocktails and mingle. I grip Jackson's arm tightly, overwhelmed by the opulence.

"Don't be nervous. You look beautiful," he whispers reassuringly. I managed a small smile in return.

Jackson guides me gracefully around the room, introducing me as his blushing bride-to-be. I play the part as we practiced - demure smiles, adoring gazes, effusive praise of him as a partner.

Despite the circumstances, Jackson himself keeps me grounded. His subtle touches and stolen glances when no one is watching remind me that our history goes far beyond this spectacle. Without him, I could never pull this off.

After greeting countless elite members of Savannah society, we finally approach a couple I recognize from portraits in Jackson's study - his parents. My stomach drops. This is the moment of truth.

"Mother, Father - allow me to introduce my fiancée, Emma Turner," Jackson announces proudly. "Emma, this is my mother, Eleanor, and my father, Jack, Sr."

His father, an older, stately version of Jackson himself, kisses my hand ceremonially. "A pleasure to meet you, my dear. Jackson tells me you've been caring for our precious Lily."

I nod graciously. "Yes sir. She's brought so much joy into my life this past year."

But his mother's eyes scrutinize me coolly, barely concealing her displeasure. She offers me the rehearsed air kisses of polite society. "What a...delightful surprise. Tell me darling, where do your family hail from?"

I falter slightly beneath her penetrating stare. "Oh, just a small rural town close-by, ma'am, nothing noteworthy."

We make polite small talk, but the undertone of judgment in her questions leaves me unsettled. As they move on to mingle with other elite guests, I feel her harsh stare following me as if to say I don't belong.

Jackson gives my hand a reassuring squeeze, grounding me amidst the turbulence. I cling to him like a life raft in this strange sea of wealth and superficial pleasantries that masks an impenetrable social hierarchy.

At dinner, I worry I'll commit some faux pas with the array of unfamiliar utensils before me. But Jackson subtly guides me, helping me navigate this foreign world.

"So when is the wedding?" Jackson's mother suddenly declares. "I insist upon hosting the ceremony at our estate of course. Only the best for our son."

I nearly choke on my wine, unprepared for talk of actual nuptials. Jackson jumps in, "Let's not get ahead of ourselves, Mother. For now, Emma and I are just enjoying our new engagement bliss."

His mother appears ready to protest, but just then the servers emerge with dessert - an ornate confection of curls, flowers, and edible gold leaf. The distraction provides momentary relief, but I know the scrutiny is far from over.

The rest of the evening passes in a haze of dancing, laughing politely at bawdy toasts, and meeting countless distinguished guests. Through it all, Jackson stays loyally by my side, our pretended affection shielding me from callous curiosity.

Finally, the end arrives and Jackson retrieves my wrap before leading me outside. In the silence of the town car, we both released a deep breath neither of us realized we were holding. It's over, the performance is done. On the ride home, Jackson squeezes my hand. "You were absolute perfection tonight," he says sincerely. And I know the real man beside me now is the only part that matters.

Jackson

As I lay restless in bed, scenes from the previous night's gala kept replaying through my mind. I couldn't forget the way the glittering chandeliers had illuminated the ballroom with an artificial brightness that failed to touch Emma's eyes. Their usual lively sparkle had been clouded by hurt I wished desperately to erase.

Thoughts of Emma consumed me - the sound of her warm laughter, her smile that never failed to lift my spirits, our long conversations whispering secrets under starry skies. Being with her was like a sanctuary, a shelter from the imposing world of manners and expectations that had shaped my upbringing.

When I finally accepted that sleep would continue evading me, I rose with determination, quickly dressing and slipping out into the predawn stillness. The rumble of the car engine coming to life punctuated the silence as I set off to confront the root of Emma's discomfort - my mother.

As I approached the looming family mansion, generations of tradition clung to its imposing stone facade, the ivy creeping upward a fitting symbol of expectations creeping into all aspects of our privileged lives. I found Mother seated in the garden, surrounded by the cloying sweetness of overflowing blossoms that contrasted sharply with the bitter seeds of discontent churning within me.

We exchanged cordial greetings, but I did not dance around the purpose of my visit today. I dove directly into an impassioned defense of my relationship with Emma, fueled by the image of hurt marring her usually cheerful expression.

Mother responded as expected, with polite platitudes and softly dismissive remarks about Emma's suitability. But I could read the truth in her eyes - she did not approve of my affection for a woman of humbler means. Mother's thin social smile had barely concealed her distaste for Emma's simpler origins the night before.

I thought back to stolen moments with Emma, laughing freely over steaming mugs at a cozy diner downtown she'd introduced me to - one of those places my elite circle would never deign to enter.

How starkly those joyful memories contrasted with the rigid perfection my mother sought to uphold. Her sterile parsley-garnished world felt so far removed from the authentic moments where Emma and I had found genuine happiness in each other. I longed to make Mother understand that.

So I unleashed the full passion of my conviction, my pleas for acceptance echoing disruptively through the carefully curated tranquility of the garden landscape. I witnessed the subtle hardness that entered Mother's eyes, the nearly invisible tightening of her mouth that signaled she would not be swayed.

As she responded with examples of her own dutiful sacrifices, memories of wealth and reputation preserved through stifling tradition, I was struck by a long-forgotten scene from my childhood. I had once overheard my parents arguing late into the night after a business deal fell through, prompting fears of social consequences and scandal.

I remember Mother consoling my distraught father, whispering about the burdens and expectations inherent to their elite social position. She had urged him to bear the discomfort of pretense and propriety, sacrificing authenticity for the preservation of our family's stature.

It dawned on me then that in Mother's mind, she was protecting the Thornfield legacy - our influence, status, and power. It was a gilded cage built to elevate us above the uncultured masses. Love, connection, fulfillment - those were merely sentimental notions compared to the duties of our ancestry.

But Emma had shown me a different path, where love flowed freely unencumbered by social standings or wealth. With her, status was irrelevant. She offered a future where I could find genuine joy and purpose. Where happiness wasn't sacrificed at the altar of keeping up appearances or pretentious pursuits.

My heart pounded as I held Mother's gaze, willing her to truly see me, and to understand the sincerity and depth of my love for Emma. I noticed her posture, rigidly controlled with generations of etiquette embedded into every carefully measured movement. But I had not come here for decorum. I came to stand up for what - and who - my heart treasured.

"I love her, Mother," I stated simply and directly, the words tremulous but filled with conviction.

Eleanor blinked rapidly as though shaking off an unpleasant thought, the perpetually polite mask she wore shifting minutely. "Jackson, you've always been one to lead with your heart," she replied gently. "But love, especially for those in our position, is far more...complicated."

I vehemently rejected that notion. What was complicated was the endless navigation of proper appearances - the garden luncheons, society galas, and schmoozing with elite connections.

Loving Emma felt like the most natural, honest thing I had ever experienced.

We discussed the differences in our backgrounds, Mother warning that Emma's world could be equally harsh and unforgiving in its own way. But I didn't care about petty social divisions. I wanted her to welcome Emma, not where she came from.

When Eleanor questioned my duties to the family empire and business, I promised I would not fully abandon those responsibilities. But I refused to pretend any longer, sacrificing my chance at happiness and fulfillment to satisfy archaic expectations.

A solitary tear escaping was the only indication of Eleanor's shifting emotional state. She asked poignantly if I would still follow our prescribed path should she be unable to adjust her perspective. My heart ached, but my resolve remained firm - this was my choice to make, and it felt true.

In the end, Mother and I had reached a tentative understanding. We stood among the roses, their delicate petals contrasting our thorny discussion. Yet seeing slivers of change in Eleanor's stoic armor gave me hope.

As I bid her an emotional goodbye, her parting words were to wish Emma could make me happy. I assured her sincerely that Emma was my guiding light, my truest joy. For the first time, I left my mother with a lightness in my step rather than a heavy heart.

Driving away, my thoughts danced with visions of a shared future unfettered by family legacy or social standings. Emma was my sanctuary - in her arms, I had faith we could find simple but profound fulfillment, beyond superficial pursuits. Our love would flourish, far from the world that could never truly comprehend its boundless depth. I just hoped that Emma felt the same way.

Emma

As Emma rested her forehead against the cool window pane, images from the past fluttered through her mind, presenting moments spent with Jackson in a nostalgic slideshow. She recalled the innocent beginnings of their relationship. The stark business arrangement with her as his daughter's nanny.

She remembered a particular evening, during their rehearsals for the fake engagement, while sitting outside by the ocean, the world dipped in a peaceful silence, save for the soft susurrous of the waves breaking on the shore and the whisper of the night wind. Jackson's eyes had met hers, and for a moment, time seemed to stand still. His fingers gently brushed against hers, a silent but profound question hanging between them. It was a moment teetering on the precipice of change, a moment that hinted at more than friendship.

Emma's heart raced as she recollected the sensation of his hand enveloping hers, a warm reassurance amidst the cascading doubts within her mind. She had pulled back then, a quiet fear wrapping its fingers around her heart, whispering warnings of change, of lost friendships, and potential heartbreak.

Love was a gamble, a leap into the unknown. She and Jackson had something beautiful, something unspoken yet deeply understood between them. Admitting to deeper, more profound feelings was a step towards a future unknown, and Emma was terrified of tarnishing the beautiful canvas of their friendship with the chaotic splatters of romantic entanglements.

Yet, as she reeled through their memories, she couldn't ignore the undeniable truth that whispered from every recollection, every stolen glance, and every lingering touch – she loved him, wholly and completely.

Emma blinked away the tears, gazing at her reflection in the glass, the vulnerability in her eyes gazing back at her, raw and unfiltered. She loved Jackson. Those three words, so simple yet immeasurably complex, held the power to either weave a beautiful tapestry of shared futures or sever the threads that had so intricately bound them together.

She found herself at a crossroads, a place where one path led to the safety of the known, and the other ventured into the realms of heartfelt confessions and shared dreams. Her love for Jackson was like a gentle flame, warming her from the inside, and the thought of suppressing it, of hiding it away, felt like a disservice to her heart.

Emma sighed, her reflection merging with the horizon, where the setting sun kissed the day goodbye, promising hope for the morrow. Tomorrow - a world where maybe, just maybe, her love for Jackson could bloom freely, unburdened by fears and what-ifs.

Embracing her truth, Emma knew she needed to step into the future with honesty, not just for her sake, but for Jackson's, even if it meant venturing into the unknown, where their friendship could either blossom into something more beautiful or wither into lost potential.

The next morning, Emma's fingers idly traced the smooth surface of the tea cup, her mind a whirlpool of thoughts, primarily centered around the evening prior. The gala, a dizzying maze of smiles, laughs, and subtleties, still lingered in her thoughts, primarily the moments shared with Eleanor, Jackson's mother.

She thought back to the way Eleanor's eyes, polite yet distant, dissected her, sizing her up against a checklist Emma was sure she did not meet. The petite, unspoken judgments whispered in politely veiled comments, Eleanor's body language, it was all imprinted in her memory.

Emma sighed, shifting her gaze towards the window, observing the way the light filtered through the curtains, drawing patterns on the floor. She saw herself there, caught between light and shadow, clear and obscured, known and misunderstood.

It was true, she wasn't born into wealth or status, her life previously didn't include galas, ornate dresses, or polite society where a single misplaced word could spell scandal. Her upbringing was modest, her family, while not wealthy in possessions, was rich in love and understanding.

But Emma knew the value she brought - her genuine spirit, her steadfast loyalty, and a love for Jackson that was as deep and endless as the ocean. The thought of him warmed her, a beacon amidst the remnants of chilly glances and veiled words. He was her safe harbor, her peaceful solace, and she was determined to not let misunderstandings erode their happiness.

She contemplated, analyzing her emotions and thoughts, sifting through them to find a resolution. Should she reach out to Eleanor, strive to clear the misunderstandings, and offer an olive branch of sorts? Her instincts told her to fight, not with aggression but with openness, to lay bare her intentions, her love for Jackson, and let Eleanor see the truth without veils or pretenses.

And so, with a soft exhale, Emma rose, her decision made. It was not just for her, not just for Jackson, but for a future, potentially punctuated with family gatherings, Christmases, and grandkids. The prospect of becoming a part of Jackson's family, Eleanor included, hung in the balance, and she was willing to fight for a place at the table.

She took a moment to reflect, to gather her thoughts, and prepare herself for what lay ahead. It wasn't about convincing Eleanor to like her, it was about showing her that she, despite all their differences, loved Jackson unconditionally.

Emma picked up her phone, her fingers lightly tapping against the screen as she typed a message to Eleanor, requesting a meeting, a chance to talk, woman to woman, heart to heart.

She could only hope that Eleanor would be willing to listen, to really hear her, and see beyond the surface. With bated breath, she awaited a response, a decision that could potentially bridge their worlds or further deepen the divide.

Emma stood hesitantly at Eleanor's door, her heart fluttering anxiously within her chest. The grandeur of the residence, an embodiment of Eleanor's dignified poise, stood as a silent observer of the unfolding drama.

When Eleanor welcomed her, there was no sign in her eyes of the confrontation she'd had with Jackson earlier that day. Her expression was a calm ocean, hiding beneath its surface the turmoil of thoughts and reflections spurred by her son's fervent words.

Emma took a breath, steadying herself before she ventured into the depths of her own vulnerability. "Eleanor, I wanted to talk to you. Just us, woman to woman."

Eleanor, graceful as always, led her into a meticulously decorated sitting room, where generations of family memories adorned the walls, watching over them as silent spectators to this crucial encounter. The two women sat, an unspoken tension mingling with the faint scent of Eleanor's floral perfume.

My heart hammered in my chest, each beat echoing a tremor of nervous energy through my veins as I gazed into Eleanor's discerning eyes. Her posture, dignified and reserved, posed a silent contrast to the chaos of emotions roiling inside of me. Her home, a manifestation of a world steeped in tradition and affluence, was a far cry from the humble, warm abode of my upbringing.

"I care deeply for Jackson, Eleanor," my voice, though steadier than I felt inside, was a mere whisper in the expansive elegance of the room.

Her eyebrows lifted subtly, a silent invitation to continue, to peel away the layers I had so carefully wrapped around my feelings.

As I plunged into the depths of my confession, a cascade of memories enveloped me. Jackson, with his easy smile and gentle eyes, had unknowingly become the keeper of my heart. It was an emotional terrain I'd navigated silently, holding my love for him like a secret, pressed close to my chest.

"I love him," the words, simple yet seismic, slipped into the space between us, "And it has nothing to do with status or wealth, Eleanor."

My words formed from a place within me that was pure, unburdened by the specter of material gain or social climbing. I carried on, baring the core of my feelings in front of Jackson's mother. "My feelings for him are rooted in something far deeper, in the person he is when the world isn't watching, in the kindness that isn't written up in newspapers."

Eleanor remained a statue, her expression meticulously neutral, revealing nothing of the thoughts that might be weaving behind her stoic gaze.

My hands, intertwined tightly in my lap, became the sole visible testament to the vulnerability cascading through me. "My background, my lack of lineage or inheritance, doesn't detract from the truth and sincerity of my emotions," I whispered, a silent plea for understanding threading through my words.

In this meticulously appointed room, where every artifact spoke of generations of privilege and lineage, I, a woman of simple means, had laid my heart bare, not with desperation, but with the strength drawn from genuine, unbridled love.

"I see him, truly see him, Eleanor," I continued, my voice a mere breath, "and I love the man I see. I didn't come from where you did, Eleanor. My world was small, modest, but it was bound together by love, sincere and unpretentious. My parents taught me that wealth isn't measured by material possessions, but by the moments we share, the love we give and receive.

I love Jackson, Eleanor." my voice, quiet but laden with unspoken emotions. A silence lingered between us, a delicate space where understanding began to bloom. "I'm not asking for your approval, Eleanor, but for your understanding."

Eleanor, perceiving the genuine emotion emanating from Emma, found herself traversing through her own emotional landscape, where maternal protectiveness encountered empathetic understanding.

She saw, perhaps for the first time, not an imposter or a threat, but a woman, sincere and unassuming, laying her emotions bare with no expectation of reciprocity.

Eleanor's voice, gentle yet heavy with emotion, broke the silence, "Emma, I see you, and I hear you."

In that moment, shared between lingering fragilities and unveiled truths, two worlds collided, paving the way for an unexpected but profoundly needed understanding.

Jackson

My mind reeled as I drove back from the fraught conversation with my mother. Her final words kept echoing through me - "I hope she makes you happy." I knew how much those words had cost Mother, whose worldview was so fundamentally different from Emma's. Yet in that moment, seeing past their differences to find understanding, my poised, proper mother had surprised me.

But now, as I ventured into the familiar space, everything felt different. I was not the same man who had left these rooms earlier; my emotions, my future plans – all had shifted.

I called her name, "Emma," letting it linger in the quiet house. But there was no response, only the distant echo of my own voice, amplifying the emptiness around me. My brow furrowed in concern. She had been in my thoughts throughout the confrontation with my mother, a steady source of warmth and resolve. Now, I needed to see her, to be in her comforting presence.

Moments later, the front door creaked open, and her voice, a familiar, soothing melody, danced through the air. My body instinctively turned toward her, my heart recognizing her presence before my eyes could confirm it.

Emma, with her eyes gleaming with a mix of emotions, approached. "Jackson," she breathed my name like a whispered secret, "we need to talk."

And so, we sank into a conversation that was an outpouring of truths, revelations about our visits to my mother, and the raw, unspoken feelings that had silently woven through our time together. Our words, gentle and sincere, unveiled the love that had quietly blossomed between us.

"I love you, Emma," the words, simple, yet laden with meaning, escaped my lips, bridging the gap between unsaid emotions and a future yet to be written.

As Emma's eyes glistened with unshed tears, she whispered back, "I love you too, Jackson."

I froze, disbelief and elation warring within me. Emma loved me. Me! Not the wealthy scion, the newspaper headlines, the polished veneer - but Jackson, just as I was.

Seeing me speechless, Emma pressed on, her voice soft but sure. "I've loved you for so long, but fear held me back. I was scared of changing us, of losing my job if things didn't work out."

Emma moved closer, her hand coming up to cradle my cheek. "You're my safe place, Jack. Loving you feels like coming home."

Hearing my nickname, so casually intimate on Emma's lips, broke me from my stunned silence. Gripping her hand, I brought it to my lips, kissing her palm reverently.

"Emma, my Emma..." I rasped, emotion cracking my voice. "You have no idea how long I've wanted to hear you say those words. I never dreamed you could love me back."

Joy shone through Emma's teary smile. "How could I not love you? You see me, really see me in a way no one else does."

Reluctantly pulling back, I knew I had to share about my mother too. "I spoke to my mother today. About you, about us. She...she gave us her blessing, Emma."

Emma nodded, some of the tension easing from her face. "It's a good first step. We'll figure the rest out together." She leaned up on her toes, nose brushing mine. "One day at a time right?"

Our lips met in a kiss that was a tender collision of all the unsaid words, unshed tears, and unexplored futures that lay ahead of us. It was a kiss that spoke of promises, understanding, and a love that had quietly grown amidst shared glances and gentle touches.

The world faded, and for a moment, we were enveloped in a bubble where nothing else existed but us, our shared heartbeat echoing a gentle lullaby of love and promise.

Then, a delicate giggle pierced our secluded world, a sound so sweet and innocent, we instinctively broke apart, turning toward the source of the unexpected mirth.

Lily, her eyes wide and sparkling with mischief and joy, stood there, her tiny hands clapping in untamed delight. "Daddy, Miss Emma, kissy!" she cheered, a beaming smile lighting up her little face.

My six year old took in our disheveled state and grinned. "You were KISSING." She drew out the word with childish glee.

"Lily! We, uh, didn't realize you were home," I ruffled my daughter's hair, embarrassment coloring my cheeks.

"We were just..." Emma trailed off, smiling sheepishly.

"K-I-S-S-I-N-G!" Lily sing-songed, before collapsing into giggles. Emma and I looked at each other, the absurdity of being caught making out by my little girl hitting us both. Soon all three of us dissolved into laughter.

Scooping Lily up, I planted a sloppy kiss on her cheek. "Alright you little rascal, no more teasing." I shot Emma a smile over Lily's head. "Emma and I were talking about some grown up stuff."

Lily scrunched her nose. "Grown ups are weird." Wriggling out of my arms, she grabbed both our hands. "Come play dolls with me!"

Allowing ourselves to be tugged along by the imperious child, Emma and I shared a look brimming with tenderness. The innocence of Lily's delighted abandon was a balm, soothing away the last lingering anxieties.

Later, after Lily was tucked into bed, Emma curled up beside me on the porch swing. My arm wrapped securely around her shoulders as we gently swayed under the starry sky.

"Quite a day, huh?" I murmured, dropping a kiss to Emma's hair.

She snuggled closer with a contented hum. "Best day ever. My secret's out now - I'm absolutely crazy about you Jackson Thornfield."

My heart swelled as I tipped Emma's chin up. "I've never loved anyone the way I love you."

Our lips met softly this time, the frenetic passion from earlier tempered into sweet affection. Pulling back slightly, I rasped playfully "Now, where were we before we were so rudely interrupted?"

Emma giggled, lightly smacking my chest before melting into another lingering kiss. Under the moonlight we traded leisurely caresses and whispered endearments, our new love burning bright.

Then I looked into her eyes, questioningly, and her response was a nod. Hand in hand we headed into the house and to my bedroom.

Emma

As Jackson leaned in to kiss me, I felt my heart racing. This was it. The moment of truth.

But as his lips met mine, I felt a surge of desire wash over me. It was like all the fear and uncertainty I had been feeling melted away in the heat of the moment.

Jackson's hand slid up my thigh, his fingers trailing along the hem of my dress. I moaned into his mouth, the taste of desire on my tongue.

He pulled back and looked at me, his eyes dark with passion. "Are you sure?" he asked, his voice husky with need.

I nodded, my hands reaching up to pull him in for another kiss. The heat between us was undeniable, and I knew this was what I wanted.

When we reached the top of the stairs, Jackson lifted me and carried me to his bedroom, his hands roaming over my body as he kissed me deeply. He laid me down on the bed, his eyes never leaving mine as he stripped off his clothes.

I couldn't take my eyes off him, his chiseled abs and muscular arms tempting me beyond words. He climbed on top of me and hovered above me as he slowly slid my dress over my head.

I reached behind my back and unclasped my bra, letting it fall to the side. I was naked beneath him, but instead of feeling exposed and vulnerable, it felt right. It felt like I was supposed to be there.

Jackson lowered his lips to mine, kissing me gently. "God, you're beautiful," he whispered in my ear.

He lowered his lips to my neck, kissing my collarbone and trailing his way down my body. In a moment, I was lost in sensation, my mind consumed by the feeling of his lips against my skin.

"I need you," I breathed, my hands reaching up to pull him back down to me.

He climbed back on top of me, and I moaned as I felt his erection pressed against me. As he positioned himself against my waiting entrance, he paused and looked me in the eyes. "Are you sure?"

I nodded, my body quivering with anticipation. He grabbed my hips and positioned himself against my waiting opening.

I wrapped my legs around him and pulled him gently into me. I had waited so long for this, and I wanted him inside of me more than I had wanted anything in my life.

As he began to push into me, I felt an odd sensation as he filled me up. It was the first time I had had sex without a condom since I was in high school, but it felt so natural. It felt so right.

As he thrust into me, I wrapped my arms around his neck and pulled him into a deep, passionate kiss. It was everything I had waited for and dreamed it would be.

We rocked together, his hands bracing his weight as his lips trailed down my body, exploring every inch of my skin with his tongue. Every thrust of his cock sent me soaring higher and higher until I felt like I was floating and the world around me was melting away.

He was everywhere, his hands, his lips, his body. He was the air I breathed, and I never wanted to let him go. He was the only thing I had waited for my whole life.

Within moments, I felt my orgasm hit me, quickly followed by an intense sensation that I had never felt before. I felt like I was falling and floating simultaneously, and the sensation of a powerful and intense pleasure was taking over my body.

"Oh my God," I gasped as I came.

Jackson thrust into me faster, his hips rocking against mine as I moaned in pleasure. I could feel his body tensing and quivering as he came.

I cried out as he rocked into me, his warmth filling me up in a way I had never experienced before. I could feel it dripping as he pulled out of me and collapsed beside me.

We lay there in each other's arms until the sun began to rise and the rest of the world began to come back into focus. I smiled and laughed as he wrapped his arms around me, the two of us lost in our own little world.

I had never felt safer or happier than I did at this moment right now. I had been scared, but now it was just an afterthought.

Jackson

My heart beat rapidly in my chest as I led Emma down the winding path to the secluded beach I had discovered weeks ago. Today was the day - I was finally going to ask this extraordinary woman to marry me, for real, this time.

As we crested the grassy overlook, the sound of waves rolling gently to shore greeted us. Emma gasped in delight at the sight. "Oh Jackson, it's beautiful!" She turned to me, eyes shining. "However did you find this place?"

I just smiled, drinking in her joy. I had scouted countless hidden coves along this shoreline before discovering this perfect one - a sheltered inlet surrounded by swaying sea grasses. Knowing Emma's love of the ocean, I wanted our proposal to be unforgettable.

We strolled leisurely across the sand hand in hand, letting the surf tickle our bare feet. The salty breeze carried Emma's melodic laugh as she pointed out creatures scuttling amidst the rocks. Her childlike wonder at the treasures revealed by the receding tide never failed to warm my heart.

By unspoken agreement we meandered over to a weathered log resting higher up the beach. As we sat hip to hip gazing out at the shimmering waves, I marveled that even in silence, just being with Emma felt like coming home.

I turned slightly, just drinking in her profile haloed by the setting sun. Sensing my attention, Emma rotated towards me, eyes crinkling with affection. "Penny for your thoughts?"

I smiled, reaching out to tenderly tuck a windblown strand of hair behind her ear. "Just thinking how lucky I am. And how this feels like the perfect moment."

Emma cocked her head curiously but I just continued to stare, memorizing each beloved feature. I traced my thumb over her delicate cheekbone. "You are so beautiful. Inside and out."

My heart swelled seeing pink flush her cheeks. No matter how many times I complimented her, Emma never failed to react with touching modesty. It was just one of the countless things I adored about her.

Impulsively, I leaned in to brush my lips over hers, trying to convey with a feather-light kiss the depth and sincerity of my love. As I went to draw back, Emma made a small sound of protest, grabbing my collar to reel me in for a longer, deeper kiss.

We eventually had to part for air. Resting her forehead against mine, Emma murmured a bit breathlessly, "You seem extra affectionate this evening, Mr. Thornfield. Dare I ask what's gotten into you?"

I huffed a laugh. "You. Always you, Emma." I stroked her jaw tenderly. "From the moment we met, you've gotten into my heart, my mind...my very soul. There's no part of me left untouched by your light."

Emma's eyes looked suspiciously watery. "Jackson..." she whispered. "I feel the same. I can't imagine my life without you in it."

My own vision grew misty. This was the opening I needed. Taking a steeling breath, I shifted off the log, lowering myself to one knee in the sand before a wide-eyed Emma.

Her hands flew up to cover her mouth. "Oh my god, Jackson, are you...?"

I grinned up at her, unshed tears making her emerald eyes sparkle like jewels. Taking her delicate hands in mine, I began to speak from the heart.

"Emma Turner, you stumbled into my life one day and nothing has been the same since." I squeezed her hands gently. "Your spirit, your passion, your immense heart - everything about you has utterly and completely captivated me."

Emma let out a shaky laugh, joy and disbelief warring on her features. I pressed on. "We just fit, you and me. In a way I never dreamed possible. You challenge me, comfort me, and make every single day better just by being in it."

Releasing one of her hands to brush a stray tear from her cheek, I dropped my voice to an earnest whisper. "I want nothing more than to laugh with you, grow with you, and build a beautiful life together, full of love and family and joy."

I withdrew a small velvet box from my pocket. Emma's breath hitched as I opened it to reveal the antique diamond ring I had chosen for its unique beauty. Just like her.

"So Emma Turner, my true love - will you make me the happiest man alive by becoming my wife?"

For a suspended moment Emma just stared, eyes flicking between my hopeful face and the glittering ring. Then with a cry of "Yes, yes of course I'll marry you!" she launched herself off the log and into my arms.

We tumbled joyfully onto the sand, laughter mixing with happy tears. When we finally caught our breath, I slipped the ring onto her trembling finger. "A perfect fit," I pronounced. "Just like you and me."

Emma gazed at the ring now gracing her hand before surging up to kiss me soundly. We exchanged whispered "I love you's" between lingering caresses as the waves provided a soothing soundtrack.

Everything was absolutely perfect. Yet in my heart, I knew this was just the beginning. A whole lifetime of creating special moments together stretched ahead of us. As the setting sun painted the horizon in dazzling hues, I cradled my blissful fiancée close. No matter what our future held, we would face it hand in hand.

Now, basking in contented silence, Emma idly twisted the new ring on her finger. Noticing her distraction, I squeezed her knee gently. "Penny for your thoughts?"

Emma smiled softly. "Just thinking how perfectly today went. The beach, the sunset…you absolutely nailed the proposal I didn't even know I dreamed of."

Warmth bloomed in my chest at her obvious delight. I pressed a kiss to her temple. "All that matters is you saying yes. The rest was just window dressing."

"Window dressing I'll remember for the rest of my life," Emma countered cheekily. Then her expression grew serious. "But it wasn't just the beautiful setting. It was…" She hesitated, searching for the words.

I nudged her encouragingly. Emma exhaled slowly. "It was the way you spoke from your heart. The way you see and love every part of me." Her eyes were luminous in the fading light. "You let me know, without doubt, that we're starting an amazing adventure together."

My own throat grew tight with emotion. I tucked a strand of hair behind Emma's ear, caressing her cheek. "We are. And I promise it will only get better from here."

She turned her face into my palm, pressing a kiss there. "I believe you," Emma whispered. "As long as we face it together, I know our life will be everything we've dreamed."

Drawn like magnets, our lips met in a kiss brimming with promise. When we finally parted, my heart was overflowing with love for this remarkable woman.

Emma

Later that next evening As the sun sets on a beautiful evening, casting a warm glow across the room, We sit on the couch, my heart still brimming with joy from Jackson's proposal.

Lily sits beside me, playfully chattering about sweet nothings. I take a deep breath, preparing myself for a conversation that could shape our lives in more ways than one.

"Lily, there's something important I need to tell you," I say, my voice filled with tenderness. "Daddy proposed to me, and I said yes. We're going to get married. Are you happy about it?"

Her eyes widen with surprise, and a moment of silence hangs in the air. Then, her little face scrunches up, and in a sharp tone, she says, "No."

I feel a pang of concern and confusion. "Oh, sweetheart, why aren't you happy? Don't you want Daddy and me to get married?" I share a fleeting glance with Jackson who looks just as confused.

She shakes her head and looks down, her voice barely a whisper. "It's because I didn't participate in it. I have... I have to help daddy."

My heart melts at her innocent point of view, and I exchange another glance with Jackson. We both understand the significance of this moment for Lily, and we want her to feel included and loved.

Jackson takes a deep breath, his eyes filled with a mix of amusement and adoration. "You're absolutely right, Lily. It wouldn't be complete without you. Shall we make it special?"

Lily's face lights up with excitement, and she eagerly reaches for a notepad and pen. Her little fingers grip the pen tightly as she carefully writes her message. When she finishes, she hands it to Jackson with a smile.

I watch as he unfolds the note, and he smiles. "Are you ready?"

"Wait, daddy." She runs into her room and comes back with a plastic ring she had found in a cereal box, giggling gleefully. "You will need a ring too, like they do in the movies."

"Wow, Lily. That's very thoughtful. Thanks, honey." Jackson gives her a high-five, then turns to me and hands me Lily's handwritten note which reads, "Will you marry Daddy?"

Jackson clears his throat and begins, "Emma, my love, I propose to you again, this time with Lily's blessing. Will you marry me and become not only my partner but also the mother to our incredible Lily?"

"Say yes, Miss Emma. Say yes!" Lily claps excitedly.

I nod, my heart overflowing with love and gratitude. "Yes, Jackson, a thousand times yes. I would be honored to marry you and be a part of this beautiful family."

Jackson puts the plastic ring on my finger and Lily squeals with delight, jumping into our embrace as we share a moment of pure joy.

***

The day after Jackson's heartfelt seaside proposal, wedding planning kicked into high gear. We were eager to make our union official, but also wanted to thoughtfully craft a meaningful celebration with our loved ones.

One afternoon, while finalizing ideas over tea and cake samples with my future mother-in-law Eleanor, I shyly asked if she would help bring our vision to life. Having organized high society galas for years, Eleanor's event planning expertise would be invaluable.

But it was the way her face lit up when I extended the invitation that meant even more. "Oh, Emma! I'd be absolutely delighted," she exclaimed, covering my hand with hers.

Though our backgrounds differed greatly, Eleanor and I had bonded over the one thing that mattered most - our mutual love and devotion to Jackson. Now I was welcoming her into the role of mother, cementing her place in our new little family.

From that day onward, Eleanor threw herself wholeheartedly into wedding preparations. She transformed her formal sitting room into a wedding command center, with fabric swatches, bridal magazines, and design sketches covering every surface.

For hours we would chat over tea, debating cake flavors or narrowing down centerpiece options while brainstorming ways to infuse charming, personal details. Eleanor even replicated my dream wedding bouquet, knitting together cream and blush roses from her own garden.

It was clear Eleanor wasn't simply going through the motions - she was emotionally invested. "It has to be perfect for you and Jack," she asserted, blinking back tears while caressing the delicate silk flowers she had painstakingly made.

In the weeks leading up to the big day, we grew ever closer, bridging the gap between two very different worlds. The wedding became a tapestry embroidered with both of our contributions.

On the sunny January morning I'd dreamed of, I watched Eleanor direct the florist in draping the ancient oak trees along the estate's driveway with gossamer silk ribbons and fragrant buds.

"Something old and something new," she said with a wink, squeezing my hands. My heart swelled with love for this woman who had become so much more than my fiancé's mother. She was family.

It was time.

I glimpsed little Lily ahead, skipping with joy as she scattered rose petals, while my father and I walked down the aisle. Eleanor's pleased gasp let me know all the time and care she had poured into this day had been worth it. Jackson's tears when he saw me approach in my lace-trimmed gown were the ultimate seal of approval.

Jackson and I had asked if she would be our flower girl, and Lily had taken her job very seriously, practicing for weeks. Now on the big day, her exuberance lit up the venue with delight.

Reaching the front, Lily went obediently to stand beside Eleanor. That's when my groom-to-be Jackson caught my eye and gave me a playful wink - the signal that our surprise for Lily was about to unfold.

Just as the Reverend welcomed our gathered friends and family, he kindly called Lily up to stand between me and Jackson at the altar. Her little brow crinkled in confusion, but she stepped up without hesitation. I felt Jackson give her shoulder a reassuring squeeze.

When the time came for our vows, the Reverend nodded meaningfully at us. Turning to Lily, he said, "Lily, Emma and your Dad have a very special question to ask you first."

Kneeling to Lily's level, I took one of her small hands as Jackson grasped the other. Gazing into her innocent eyes, I asked gently, "Lily, do you accept me becoming a permanent part of your family from this day forward?"

Lily's eyes went round before she nodded so enthusiastically her flower crown slipped sideways. "Yes!" she cried, barreling into me for a fierce hug that I returned joyfully. I smoothed down her mussed hair, my heart overflowing.

"Well then, let's proceed!" the Reverend proclaimed with a broad grin. As he led Jackson and I through our heartfelt vows of lifelong love and commitment, I knew with certainty we both meant every word.

When the Reverend finally closed his book, he announced with a twinkle in his eye, "You may now kiss your family!"

Grinning widely, my new husband and I leaned down to plant a sweet kiss on our giggling flower girl's rosy cheeks. When applause erupted, we turned and gathered a teary Eleanor into our embrace too.

In that moment, with my new little family encircled in my arms, I was positive our joyous union could not have started off on a more beautiful note than this.

The reception afterward could not have gone more perfectly, thanks to Eleanor's diligent planning and attention to detail. She made sure our joyous union received the celebration it deserved.

Swaying in my new husband's arms amidst the twinkle lights on the dance floor, I felt utterly content. Jackson must have sensed my soaring happiness. "You look radiant, my bride," he murmured before kissing me tenderly.

Across the room, I caught Eleanor's glistening gaze observing us. I smiled and mouthed a heartfelt "Thank you!" Her proud, pleased nod in return confirmed that a special new bond had been forged through the magic of bringing our wedding dreams to life.

Later, Eleanor took the microphone to offer a touching toast. Dabbing at her eyes delicately with a monogrammed handkerchief, she welcomed me to the family before addressing her son.

"Jack, seeing the love between you and Emma reminds me so much of the early days with your father." Her voice wavered slightly with emotion. "This bride of yours is truly special. Always cherish and nurture what you have found together."

Jackson squeezed my hand, then crossed the room in long strides to envelop his mother in a hug. My own eyes grew misty at this public display confirming I was now Eleanor's daughter too. She had embraced me as one of her own.

In the end, it was not the beautiful setting or delicious cuisine that made our celebration remarkable. It was the people - and one person especially. Eleanor's generous spirit, guidance, and excitement transformed our wedding into a deeply meaningful milestone surrounded in beauty.

The mother-son dance was her final gift. I will never forget the sight of Eleanor resting her head contentedly on Jackson's shoulder as they slowly revolved, her smile communicating a silent yet profound joy.

My heart overflowed with gratitude for the woman who had so lovingly helped us step into our new life together. Eleanor's support was the greatest gift, one I will always treasure. Our wedding day simply could not have been more perfect thanks to her.

Prologue

Emma - one year later

I awoke to rays of sunlight streaming into our bedroom, filling me with a sense of warmth and hope. As I shifted, Jackson's arm around my waist pulled me closer and I nestled into his strong embrace, cherishing these quiet moments. My hand drifted down to rest on my still-flat stomach as joy rushed through me. I was pregnant with our first child!

Wanting to make this morning extra special, I slipped from bed to surprise my wonderful husband with all his favorite breakfast foods. My heart fluttered imagining his reaction to the news that we were going to be parents. There was so much blissful planning ahead!

When Jackson wandered sleepily into the kitchen, he was stunned by the feast I had prepared. After we ate, I could hardly contain my exhilaration a moment longer. Taking his hands, I shared the amazing news - we were going to have a baby!

Jackson whooped joyfully and twirled me around before cradling me close. His eyes shone with happy tears as he pressed his hand to my belly in awe - we had created new life together. We spent the morning kissing and making plans, giddy with excitement.

In the days that followed, we had fun coming up with creative ways to reveal my pregnancy to Lily and Eleanor. Their enthusiasm when we surprised them with the news at dinner that weekend warmed my heart. Jackson was right, Lily was absolutely over the moon at becoming a big sister.

As my body changed and our child grew within me, I fell even more in love with my little family. Jackson was by my side at every step, caring for me so tenderly. Lily showered me with pictures and hugs for the baby. My heart overflowed.

When the big day finally arrived, the arduous hours of labor were all worth it the moment I held our beautiful son Asher for the first time. Seeing Lily meet her new baby brother was incredible. I had never felt more blessed.

Our home was filled with joy those first weeks as loved ones came to celebrate Asher's arrival. My favorite moments were the sleepy cuddles and midnight feeds, bonding with our tiny miracle. I would gaze into his innocent eyes and my heart would melt all over again.

Watching Jackson with our children, knowing we had so much love and life ahead together, I truly felt I had found my happily ever after. This family we had built was everything I never knew I needed, and always wanted. I couldn't wait to see what adventures our future held.

Don't miss out!

Visit the website below and you can sign up to receive emails whenever Lilly Grace Nash publishes a new book. There's no charge and no obligation.

https://books2read.com/r/B-A-WUJHB-UAIGD

BOOKS 2 READ

Connecting independent readers to independent writers.

Also by Lilly Grace Nash

SEALs of Love Romance
Undercover Hearts

Standalone
Alliances & Betrayals
Billionaire's Nanny Fake Marriage

Watch for more at https://lillygracenash.com.